The Boxcar Children® Mysteries

The Boxcar Children
Surprise Island
The Yellow House Mystery
Mystery Ranch
Mike's Mystery
Blue Bay Mystery
The Woodshed Mystery
The Lighthouse Mystery
Mountain Top Mystery
Schoolhouse Mystery
Caboose Mystery
Houseboat Mystery
Snowbound Mystery
Tree House Mystery
Bicycle Mystery
Mystery in the Sand
Mystery Behind the Wall
Bus Station Mystery
Benny Uncovers a Mystery
The Haunted Cabin Mystery
The Deserted Library Mystery
The Animal Shelter Mystery
The Old Motel Mystery
The Mystery of the Hidden Painting
The Amusement Park Mystery
The Mystery of the Mixed-Up Zoo
The Camp Out Mystery
The Mystery Girl
The Mystery Cruise
The Disappearing Friend Mystery

The Mystery of the Singing Ghost
The Mystery in the Snow
The Pizza Mystery
The Mystery Horse
The Mystery at the Dog Show
The Castle Mystery
The Mystery on the Ice
The Mystery of the Lost Village
The Mystery of the Purple Pool
The Ghost Ship Mystery
The Mystery in Washington DC
The Canoe Trip Mystery
The Mystery of the Hidden Beach
The Mystery of the Missing Cat
The Mystery at Snowflake Inn
The Mystery on Stage
The Dinosaur Mystery
The Mystery of the Stolen Music
The Mystery at the Ballpark
The Chocolate Sundae Mystery
The Mystery of the Hot Air Balloon
The Mystery Bookstore
The Pilgrim Village Mystery
The Mystery of the Stolen Boxcar
Mystery in the Cave
The Mystery on the Train
The Mystery at the Fair
The Mystery of the Lost Mine
The Guide Dog Mystery
The Hurricane Mystery

The Pet Shop Mystery
The Mystery of the Secret Message
The Firehouse Mystery
The Mystery in San Francisco
The Niagara Falls Mystery
The Mystery at the Alamo
The Outer Space Mystery
The Soccer Mystery
The Mystery in the Old Attic
The Growling Bear Mystery
The Mystery of the Lake Monster
The Mystery at Peacock Hall
The Windy City Mystery
The Black Pearl Mystery
The Cereal Box Mystery
The Panther Mystery
The Mystery of the Queen's Jewels
The Mystery of the Stolen Sword
The Basketball Mystery
The Movie Star Mystery
The Mystery of the Black Raven

THE MYSTERY OF THE BLACK RAVEN

created by
GERTRUDE CHANDLER WARNER

Illustrated by Charles Tang

ALBERT WHITMAN & Company
Morton Grove, Illinois

Library of Congress Cataloging-in-Publication Data

Warner, Gertrude Chandler, 1890-1979
The mystery of the black raven/
created by Gertrude Chandler Warner;
illustrated by Charles Tang.
p. cm. — (The Boxcar Children mysteries)
Summary: The Aldens investigate a mystery involving a legendary mining
expedition to the gold fields of Alaska.
ISBN 0-8075-2988-5(hardcover)—
ISBN 0-8075-2989-3(paperback)
[1.Brothers and sisters—Fiction. 2. Orphans—Fiction.
3. Alaska—Fiction. 4. Mystery and detective stories.]
I. Tang, Charles, ill. II. Title.
III. Series: Warner, Gertrude Chandler, 1890-
Boxcar children mysteries.
PZ7.W244Mth 1999   98-54886
[Fic]—dc21   CIP
                                                        AC

Cover art by David Cunningham.

Contents

CHAPTER   PAGE

1. Grandfather's Secret   1
2. The Ghost of the Golden North   16
3. "One of Us Is a Thief!"   31
4. Mystery Within a Mystery   44
5. Miss Parker's Clue   56
6. Panning for Gold   69
7. The Missing Scrapbook   82
8. Great-uncle Edward's Message   94
9. The Raven Speaks   108
10. Benny's Mystery Within a
    Mystery   120
    Perplexing Puzzle Pages   137

THE MYSTERY OF THE BLACK RAVEN

CHAPTER 1

Grandfather's Secret

Benny Alden leaned against the rail of the ferry. He threw bread crumbs at the swooping gulls. One gull almost landed on the rail next to him.

"Whoa!" Jessie, his older sister, gently pulled Benny back. "I bet that bird is as hungry as you are!" At twelve, Jessie was always looking out for her six-year-old brother.

"I am hungry, but I wanted to feed the birds first," said Benny.

"Ready for lunch?" Jessie asked. Just then

a spray of bracing sea mist stung their faces, making them laugh.

"You bet!" Benny followed Jessie across the ferry deck and into the warm dining cabin.

"There you are," said Henry. He was fourteen, the oldest of the Alden children. "We ordered hot chocolate."

"Thanks," said Jessie. "Brrr! It's cold out there!"

James Alden, the children's grandfather, nodded. "It usually is on the water, even in the spring. This far north, it rarely gets hot. Not like back home in Connecticut."

Violet, who was ten, watched seabirds flying past the large square windows. "I can't believe we'll be in Alaska in just a little while!" She patted the camera bag hanging on the back of her chair. "I plan to take lots of pictures."

"I hope I see a polar bear," said Benny. He was trying to read the menu. He didn't know many words, but he could read *hamburger* and *ice cream*.

Grandfather chuckled. "I doubt we'll see

one in Skagway. Polar bears live farther north."

"Skagway!" Benny laughed. "What a funny name!"

Their waiter came by their table. "Alaska is full of odd names," he said, setting down mugs of hot chocolate. "Skagway was once just a shack owned by a man named Moore. But then the sourdoughs came and called the place Skagway, after the Skagway River."

"Sourdoughs?" asked Jessie. "Isn't that a bread?"

The waiter nodded. "Yes. The early prospectors made that bread in the mining camps. Life was hard for those tough old gold hunters. That's why people called them sourdoughs."

"Gold hunters?" Benny said with awe. "I want to hunt gold!"

"Let's eat first," Grandfather said after ordering burgers for all.

"And wait for our ferry to dock in Skagway," Violet said. "You won't find much gold until we get to Alaska!"

So far it had been a whirlwind trip. First they flew from their home in Greenfield, Connecticut, to Seattle, Washington. That was all the way across the country! Then they took a bus to Bellingham. Big boats, little boats, and ferries were anchored at the pier in the port city.

"I like this ferry," Benny remarked when their food arrived. He bit into the juicy burger. "It's like our boxcar. Only with a boat on the bottom."

"That's a good observation, Benny," Henry said. "The ferry *is* like a floating boxcar."

The Alden children never forgot their first home. Their parents had died and they were alone. They had heard about a grand-father, but were afraid he was mean. So they found an empty boxcar in the woods and lived in it.

Then Grandfather found *them*. He wasn't mean at all, but kind and very glad to have four grandchildren. He brought the boxcar to his big house in Greenfield. Since then, the children had had many adventures.

And now they were starting a new one.

"Tell us again why we're going to Alaska," Violet said excitedly. She loved Grandfather's stories.

"Many years ago my great-uncle Edward Alden came here to be a prospector," began Grandfather. "When gold was discovered, thousands of people caught 'gold fever.' "

"Were they sick?" Benny wanted to know.

Henry shook his head. "That's just an expression."

"People were in a fever to find gold," Grandfather added. "Edward worked as a clerk in the family business. He was a young man who craved excitement. So he took a train to Seattle and then boarded a boat to Skagway."

"Just like we're doing," Jessie commented.

"Only Edward's boat was loaded with hundreds of passengers who wanted to find gold, too," Grandfather continued. "On the boat, Edward met two other men. They became friends. When they landed in Skagway, the little town was jammed with people! Edward and his new friends met another man. The four decided to stick together."

"Did they find gold?" asked Violet.

"Yes, they did," replied Grandfather. "But they had to walk a long way to the goldfields. Then they had to find enough gold in one place to stake a claim. When they found gold, they marked their claim with four rocks, so no one else could dig at their spot. My great-uncle carried a camera with him. He also kept a diary. When the men finished working their claim, they headed back to Skagway."

"I wouldn't have left," Benny put in. "I would have dug and dug till I found all the gold in the world!"

"You would have been pretty tired of the cold," said Grandfather. "And the hard work."

"What happened when the men got to Skagway?" Jessie asked.

"They turned in their gold for cash," Grandfather replied. "Then the Four Rock

Miners, as they called themselves, went home."

"Were they rich?" Henry wanted to know.

"I doubt it," Grandfather answered. "The men had excitement and adventure. After being a sourdough, Uncle Edward came back to his old job as a clerk in Connecticut."

"That doesn't sound very exciting," said Benny, dipping a french fry in ketchup.

Grandfather smiled. "Even though the men had to go back to their ordinary lives, they stayed in touch. Every year the Four Rock Miners met in Skagway."

"Like a family reunion," said Jessie.

"Exactly," said Grandfather. "The men talked about the time they spent in the goldfields. Year after year, they relived their adventures. It became a tradition."

A voice beside Grandfather's chair said, "And that's why we're here."

Jessie turned to see a young couple. The sandy-haired man wore khaki pants and a thick blue sweater. Next to him stood a pretty dark-haired woman. She also wore khaki pants, but her sweater was red. The color made her cheeks pink and her blue eyes bluer.

The young man had spoken. He continued, "I'm sorry to break into your conversation. But my wife and I couldn't help overhearing —"

Now Grandfather rose from his chair. "You must be Steve Wilson! I'm James Alden, Edward Alden's great-nephew."

"I figured as much," said Steve. "This is Jennifer. We've only been married a month."

Jennifer held Steve's hand. "We decided to make the reunion our honeymoon."

"How nice," said James Alden. "These are my grandchildren — Henry, Jessie, Violet, and Benny. This is the first time I've brought them to Alaska."

Benny was confused. "Are you guys going to hunt gold, too?"

Everyone laughed.

"I didn't finish explaining," said Grandfather. "You see, even after the original Four Rock Miners died, their relatives continued the tradition of meeting in Skagway."

"I'm the great-great-grandson of Frank Wilson," Steve said. "He was one of the men Edward Alden met on the boat to Alaska." Then he added, "Your grandfather wrote to each of us, setting up the reunion date."

Jennifer sat down in the empty seat next to Jessie. "I think this is so wonderful. The way the men went to Skagway every year, no matter what."

"There were four men," Henry said. "Where are the relatives of the other two?"

Grandfather signaled the waiter for the bill. "They are waiting at our hotel. We'll meet them there."

The waiter came over. "We'll be docking shortly. You might want to go see Alaska come into view, the way the old miners did."

Everyone slipped windbreakers over their sweaters and went outside on the deck. Gray waves slapped the sides of the ferry.

Benny's sharp eyes spotted land first.

"There it is!" he cried. "Alaska, here we come!"

Everyone was so excited about seeing the faraway state, they remained on deck the rest of the trip, even though it was chilly.

When the ferry docked at Skagway, the Aldens saw a huge cruise ship farther down the beach. Then they were busy hauling their luggage off the ferry. Grandfather called a taxi. The Wilsons followed in a separate cab.

"This is Broadway," their driver informed the Aldens. "It's the main street in town."

Jessie was amazed at the storefronts. "It looks like an old Western movie!"

Their driver laughed. "Skagway *was* like an old Western movie! Here you are." He pulled up in front of a rustic-looking building with a sign that read THE TOTEM LODGE.

The kids piled out of the cab. A bellhop hurried through the swinging door to take their bags.

Inside the lobby, Grandfather went over to the main desk.

"What a neat place!" Henry exclaimed.

The Totem Lodge was like a big log cabin. A real canoe with hidden lights hung overhead. Native American masks and gold-mining spades and other tools decorated the walls. Massive poles with strange carvings guarded the doorway into the dining room.

The lobby was warm, with potted plants, chairs, and drum-shaped tables scattered around. From one of those chairs, a silver-haired woman got up and approached Grandfather.

"You must be James Alden," the children heard her say. The woman, neatly dressed in green slacks and a leaf-green sweater, stuck out her hand. "I'm Madeline Parker."

"Miss Parker, I'm delighted to meet you in person!" said Grandfather. He intro-duced his grandchildren, adding, "This is their first time to Alaska."

"Mine, too," Miss Parker confessed. "I'm so thrilled. I'm a retired teacher. It's wonderful to be able to travel. By the way, I'm the great-niece of Pete Blake."

"Was he one of the old miners?" asked Violet.

"Yes. My great-uncle met the other three men in town." She held up a gray leather tote bag. "The important items are right here!"

Violet was about to ask what the important items were when Steve and Jennifer Wilson walked up to the desk to sign in. The bellhop who handled the Aldens' luggage was now stacking the Wilsons' bags nearby.

At that moment, a man, leading a woman and two teenagers, barged up to the front desk and complained loudly, "Are you the manager? Our room is cold!"

The desk clerk replied, "I'll see to your room, Mr. Pittman. Now, Mr. Wilson, if you'll just —"

"And more towels," the woman interrupted rudely. "How do you expect a family to get by on four measly towels?"

"I'll take care of it," said the clerk, "as soon as I've checked in this party."

"See to it you do," Mr. Pittman said.

The teenagers walked over to where the Alden children were waiting. Both were blond and freckled.

"Hi," said Henry. "I'm Henry. These are my sisters, Jessie and Violet. And this is my brother, Benny."

"I'm Monique," said the girl sullenly. Jessie guessed she was fifteen. "And this is my brother, Mark."

"Have you been here before?" Jessie asked. The kids acted awfully bored.

"No." Monique yawned. "Our parents dragged us here. Some stupid reunion thing."

"We're here for that, too!" said Violet.

"Yippee," Mark said. "Who cares what some old guys did in this boring place?"

Jessie and Violet looked at each other. How could anybody find Alaska *boring*?

Grandfather was tipping the bellhop, who had loaded his cart with their bags.

"Your reunion party has the entire third

floor," said the bellhop, whose name tag read HOWIE. "I'll take you to your rooms now."

Upstairs, Howie showed them into three rooms: one each for the girls and the boys. Grandfather's private room was next to the boys'.

"Now," said Grandfather. "Unpack quickly and freshen up. It'll soon be time for the second part of the tradition."

"What is that?" Benny asked.

Grandfather winked. "You'll just have to wait, Benny Alden. Grandfathers can have secrets, too!"

CHAPTER 2

The Ghost of the Golden North

"Where are we going?" asked Benny. Grandfather had instructed the children to put on their best outfits.

Henry pulled Benny's yellow sweater from his suitcase. "Jessie said to wear this with those pants." From his own suitcase, he found his navy sweater with red stripes. "All I know is, we're going someplace fancy."

There was a knock at the door. Benny opened it. His sisters were already dressed.

"You look nice," he told them.

"Thanks." Jessie was wearing a pleated blue skirt with a matching sweater.

Violet had on a pink jumper and her favorite pink-flowered blouse. "Grandfather's waiting for us downstairs."

The children flew down the steps and into the lobby. There, Grandfather was chatting with Miss Parker and the Wilsons. Everyone was dressed nicely, except for the Pittman family, who still wore jeans and sweatshirts. The Aldens had learned from Grandfather that Earl Pittman was distantly related to Harold Bell, the second man Edward Alden had met on the boat going to Skagway.

"We're too tired to dress up," whined Edie Pittman. She leaned against one of the carved poles.

"Yeah," said Mark. "What's the big deal, anyway?"

Grandfather led them all toward the front door. "You'll see," he said mysteriously.

Outside it was nearly dark. The wind was brisk off the nearby waterfront. Jessie was glad she had made everyone take a coat.

Monique walked beside her and Violet. "Where are we going?"

"I don't know," Violet replied. "It's not like Grandfather to be this mysterious."

"But he's enjoying it," Jessie said, smiling. "I can tell."

"Well, *I'm* not," Monique said sourly. "I wanted to order room service. It's cold out here."

"We're in Alaska," Violet said. "It's supposed to be cold." She wondered why the older girl only had on a sweatshirt. As Grandfather had warned them, springtime in the northernmost state could still be chilly.

They trooped down Broadway with other groups of tourists. Excitement crackled in the crisp air. Shop windows glittered with souvenirs, and old-time music bubbled from restaurants. People laughed and talked.

Grandfather stopped at the corner of Broadway and Third Street in front of a building called the Golden North Hotel.

"Here we are," declared James Alden. "This is the oldest hotel in Alaska. Every year the Four Rock Miners met here. And this is where we hold part of our reunion."

A blast of cold air swept them all inside.

Jessie gasped. Above her head arched a golden dome. The lobby was richly decorated with red velvet chairs and curved-back sofas. Antique mirrors with gilt frames hung on the walls. Heavy drapes covered the windows, but twinkling lamps in glass shades threw off an inviting glow.

"Wow!" breathed Benny. "This is the fanciest place I've ever seen!"

Grandfather laughed. "Yes, it *is* fancy. The hotel was built in 1898 during the Gilded Age, a very fancy time in our history."

"The Golden North has been restored to its original splendor," added Miss Parker. "The antiques are authentic. And it even has a ghost!"

"A ghost!" Benny exclaimed, looking around. "Where?"

"Can we eat?" Mark broke in. "Or are we going to stand around all night?"

"I believe our table is ready," Grandfather said as the headwaiter came up to them.

Their group was escorted to a large white-clothed table in the back, away from the other diners. The dining room was as grand as the lobby. Violet wished she had brought her sketchbook. She loved to draw interesting places.

Menus were passed around.

"Too expensive!" Earl Pittman complained loudly.

"Well, we won't have to eat here after tonight," James Alden told the other man. "The original miners stayed here, you know. And this is where they ate dinner."

"They weren't feeding a family of four," Earl grumbled.

"We should thank James for arranging this trip," said Miss Parker. "Making the reservations at the Totem Lodge, having this special table here."

"The Totem Lodge is cold," Edie Pittman argued. "I wish we were staying somewhere else."

"But we have the entire floor of that hotel," Miss Parker said. "It's perfect for a reunion."

Monique closed her menu with a disgusted sigh. "There isn't one single thing on here I like!"

Henry wondered why the Pittmans were so disagreeable. It seemed as if nothing pleased them. Henry certainly liked *his* food when it came — a delicious salmon burger.

Over dessert, Grandfather explained more about the purpose of the reunion.

"As I mentioned in my letters to all of you," he began, "I'm the only one of us who has been attending the reunions for some years."

"My aunt used to come," said Miss Parker. "But she's too ill for such a long journey."

Grandfather nodded. "Our relatives who have been making the trip are either too elderly or have health problems. So you all are new to the tradition."

Steve and Jennifer Wilson held hands across the table. "I love it here," said Jennifer. "It's so romantic."

"Well, we decided the trip would be our vacation," said Mrs. Pittman. "So far it hasn't been much of a vacation."

"It's dull here," put in Mark, stirring the chocolate sauce of his brownie sundae into a mess.

So what else is new? Jessie thought. She wondered why Mark ordered a sundae if he was only going to waste it.

"You won't be bored for long," Grandfather told Mark. "We have lots of activities planned."

"I want to hunt for gold," Benny said. "Just like Uncle Edward did."

Everyone laughed except the Pittmans.

"You'll have a chance to hunt for gold," Grandfather said. "Though not exactly the way Uncle Edward did. For one thing, we won't travel to the goldfields where the Four Rock Miners staked their claim. That's in the Yukon Territory."

"We'll learn more about the sourdoughs tomorrow when we take the guided tour," Miss Parker said.

Violet saw Monique elbow her brother and roll her eyes skyward. Violet suspected the two teenagers would complain all along the tour.

"It'd better be interesting," said Mrs. Pittman. "I didn't come all this way to listen to a bunch of guides."

"Yeah," said Monique. "I want to shop."

Grandfather tapped his spoon gently on his water glass to get everyone's attention.

"Ladies and gentlemen of the Four Rock Miners reunion. We have an important ceremony to perform. Ready, Miss Parker?"

"Yes, indeed!" The teacher's eyes were bright.

She was certainly having a good time, Violet noted. She leaned forward to see what would happen next.

Miss Parker brought her gray leather tote bag from under the table and put it on her lap. When she spoke, she reminded Violet of the mayor of Greenfield whenever he made the Fourth of July speech.

"I hereby pass on the Four Rock Miners' sacred mementos to this year's caretaker."

Benny whispered to Jessie, "What did she say?"

"It was just a little speech," Jessie whispered back.

Miss Parker drew two paper-wrapped bundles from her bag. One was flat and rectangular-shaped. The other was a rounded knobby lump.

"What are those?" asked Benny.

"You'll see shortly," Miss Parker answered, "since your grandfather is this year's caretaker." Her tone became serious again. "James Alden, do you hereby agree to accept and take excellent care of these items?"

"I do," Grandfather answered solemnly.

Miss Parker handed him the wrapped bundles. "Enjoy!"

Now everyone was curious, even Mark and Monique.

"What's in the packages?" asked Benny again. "Is it your birthday, Grandfather?"

James Alden laughed. "No, it's not my birthday." He unwrapped the round, lumpy bundle first.

It was a dark gray, nearly black, statue of a bird about five inches high. The bird had a large head and a thick beak. Wing feathers and other details were etched in stone.

"What an ugly statue!" commented Mrs. Pittman.

"It's a raven," replied Miss Parker. "A bird very important to the Native Americans who live up here. There are lots of raven stories in their culture."

"But why do *you* have it?" Mr. Pittman said to Grandfather. "Looks like a weird present, if you ask me."

"The other package will answer your questions," said Grandfather. He opened the rectangular bundle.

It was an old book bound in black leather. Holes had been punched in the cover. Black laces threaded through the holes held the pages.

Grandfather carefully flipped back the cover to the first page. Beneath an old photograph was some fancy writing.

Jessie, who was sitting next to him, read out loud, " 'Our Adventure in Alaska, by Edward J. Alden.' "

"This is a scrapbook made by my great-uncle Edward Alden," Grandfather told the group. "He took photos and kept a diary. When the miners left their claim, they bought this raven in Skagway as a souvenir. Then Edward made a scrapbook from his pictures and diary."

"So that's what he did with the pictures he took," said Violet. As the family photographer, she'd been curious.

Miss Parker took up the story. "The first year when they met in this very hotel, Edward showed the others the scrapbook. They decided that each year one of them would keep the raven and the scrapbook, until the next reunion. Then the items would be passed on to another member."

"That is so neat," said Jennifer Wilson, gently touching the raven.

"When their relatives started coming to Skagway, they continued the tradition of passing on the scrapbook and raven," said Grandfather. "This year, it's my turn again."

"Whose turn is it next year?" asked Mr. Pittman.

Grandfather checked a small notebook he

carried in his jacket. "The Wilsons'." Jennifer clapped her hands.

"Might've known we'd be last," Earl said to his wife, one corner of his mouth pulled down.

After passing around the scrapbook for everyone to see, it was time to return to the Totem Lodge.

Back at the lodge, Grandfather went up to the front desk. In keeping with the old-fashioned ways of the frontier town, room keys were kept on hooks behind the front desk.

Benny walked over to the large carved poles. The animals on it were funny, kind of squashed-looking. He saw a bird with a large head and a thick beak. *Is that a raven?* he wondered.

Before he could ask anyone, Mr. Pittman started arguing with the clerk again.

"Our room is too cold. And did you see about those extra towels yet?"

The Wilsons were patiently waiting to retrieve their key while the harried clerk

dealt with Mr. Pittman. Howie the bellhop was on duty at his station. He listened to the problems at the front desk but didn't move until the annoyed clerk rang his bell.

Grandfather had already received their room keys. The Aldens went up to the third floor.

"See you in the morning," Grandfather said to the children.

Benny was almost too tired to undress. It had been a long day. Just before he fell asleep, he heard voices in the hallway outside.

Jennifer and Steve Wilson were talking to someone else. Who? Then Benny knew. Howie, the bellhop. Howie was saying something about the totem poles downstairs. . . .

Then Benny drifted off to sleep.

The next morning the boys were awakened by a loud knock. It was Jessie and Violet.

"What happened?" Henry asked.

"It's Grandfather," Jessie cried. "The

scrapbook and raven statue have disappeared from his room!"

"Wow!" exclaimed Henry. "Were they stolen?"

"We don't know," Violet replied. "But Grandfather is very upset."

"I know what happened to them," said Benny. "The ghost of that fancy hotel came and took them!"

CHAPTER 3

"One of Us Is a Thief!"

Grandfather came out of his room. Worry lines creased his forehead, Violet noticed.

Across the hall, Miss Parker's door opened and she stepped out. She took one look at Grandfather and said, "What's wrong, James?"

"The scrapbook and raven are missing," he replied. "I put them on my dresser last night. This morning when I got up, they were gone!"

The children hurried over to join them.

31

"I bet the ghost took them," said Benny.

Grandfather looked at him. "What ghost?"

"The one that lives in the hotel we went to last night. Miss Parker told us about it. I think it followed us here and took your stuff," Benny stated.

"You don't really believe in ghosts, do you?" Jessie asked him gently. "That's just a story."

"Jessie's right, Benny," Miss Parker said. "Lots of old houses and buildings claim to have a ghost. It makes them seem more interesting."

Just then the Wilsons emerged from their room. Steve saw the group standing in the hall and asked, "What's going on? You guys look glum."

"The scrapbook and raven are gone," explained Violet.

"Gone?" echoed Jennifer. "How could that happen?"

Before Grandfather could answer, the door to the room where the Pittmans were staying flew open with a bang. The family was bickering about what to have for breakfast.

Earl Pittman nearly bumped into the gathering in the hall. "Hope you're not waiting for us. We plan to eat by ourselves this morning." He seemed grumpier than usual.

"That's not it," Miss Parker said to him. "The scrapbook and statue are missing from James's room."

"How can they be missing?" asked Edie Pittman.

Sighing, Mark and Monique leaned against the wall with annoyed looks on their faces.

"We'll never get to eat," muttered Mark.

"I put them on my dresser last night," said Grandfather. "I was tired and didn't look at them before going to bed. This morning they were gone. I searched my room from one end to the other. I can't find them. Nothing else was taken. Just the scrapbook and the raven."

Mr. Pittman's thick eyebrows drew together. "So what you're saying, James, is

that somebody broke into your room and took them!"

"I didn't hear a thing," James Alden admitted. "Granted, I was sleepy from the long day, but I would have heard someone break into my room."

Miss Parker put her hand on Grandfather's sleeve. "Why don't we all go down and eat. I'm sure the children are hungry."

Benny was starving. In the dining room, he ordered sourdough pancakes, bacon, eggs, and milk. He thought the pancakes would taste sour like their name, but they were delicious, especially drenched in warm maple syrup.

The discussion of the vanished scrapbook and statue continued.

"Are you sure you locked your door?" Edie Pittman asked Grandfather. "These locks are pretty flimsy."

"Positive," Grandfather replied. "Anyway, our reunion group is in all the rooms on the third floor. No one else."

Mr. Pittman's tone became suspicious. "Are you accusing one of *us* of stealing those things?"

"But why would any of us take them?" asked Henry. "Everyone gets to keep them for a year, anyway. Why steal them now?"

"Who'd want those dumb old things?" Monique put in, pushing the remains of a pancake around on her plate. "I mean, that statue. Yuck!"

Miss Parker spoke up. "Perhaps the person who took the items will return them later. The whole thing might be a mistake."

"That's what I think, too," agreed Grandfather. Henry knew his grandfather didn't like to argue. "Instead of accusing one another, let's get on with the reunion plans."

"You're right, Mr. Alden," said Jennifer. "Maybe the maid will find them when she cleans the rooms. Then everything will be all right."

"Let's meet in the lobby in fifteen minutes," said Miss Parker. "I want to see Alaska!"

"Me, too," Benny chimed in.

The group went back upstairs to get ready for a day of sightseeing.

The Alden children met briefly in Jessie

and Violet's room. Jessie made sure Benny was dressed warmly enough and that they all had coats and hats. Through the window, she could see the wind was still blowing.

"Well," Benny announced, "we've got another mystery to solve!"

"We'll have to keep our ears and eyes open for clues," Violet stated. "Those things belong to Grandfather, at least for this year. He should have them."

"We'll find them," Benny said confidently. "We're old hands at solving mysteries."

Jessie giggled. "Where did you hear that?"

"From Grandfather, when he was talking to Miss Parker," Benny replied.

"I have a feeling this is going to be a tough one," Henry predicted.

Downstairs they found Grandfather reporting the theft to the desk clerk. The clerk wrote up a report, apologizing all the while.

"I'm very sorry, sir," he said. "If the maid

finds those items, she'll bring them to me immediately, and I'll lock them up for safe-keeping."

"I'm sure you'll do your best," Grandfather said.

Henry was looking around for Howie. He didn't see the bellhop. Last night Howie was hanging around the reunion group, listening to them. Maybe it was Howie's day off.

"Where to first?" asked Steve Wilson when they had all assembled by the totem poles. He had collected a handful of brochures from a rack by the dining room.

"I want to go to the movies," said Mark.

"The *movies*!" exclaimed Jennifer. "You can go to the movies anytime. We're in Alaska!"

Mark shrugged. "So?"

"I want to go shopping," said Monique.

"I'd like to take a tour first," said Miss Parker. "To get the feel of old Alaska."

Earl Pittman held up a hand. "Wait a minute! Have we all forgotten that one of us is a thief? I think we should stick together. That way, the thief won't be able to slip off and mail the scrapbook and raven back home."

Everyone was silent.

Then Steve said, "You know, Earl, the stolen items could be in any of our suitcases. Are we going to search one another's luggage?"

Mr. Pittman's neck turned red.

"I don't believe that's necessary," Grandfather said quickly. "The items may turn up or be found by the housekeeper, as Jennifer suggested."

Jennifer nodded, adding, "I think Mr. Pittman has a good idea. About staying together, I mean. Instead of everyone running off in different directions, let's be like the Four Rock Miners."

"That's the spirit!" Grandfather said heartily, herding the group out the front door. "Let's discover Skagway!"

Their first stop was the granite City Hall building, where they gathered more information on day trips from the Visitors' Bureau. The Trail of '98 Museum was on the second floor. There they saw things such as scales for measuring gold, old photos, and Native American artifacts.

"Look," said Benny, always sharp-eyed. "There's a raven almost like ours!"

Miss Parker nodded. "You'll find the raven symbol used a great deal among the various tribes up here. One story says that the raven created the world."

"How did he do that?" asked Benny, who loved stories.

"The world was all darkness," said Miss Parker. "The raven opened a box and flew out carrying light in his beak. That light is the sun."

Next the group went to the Eagles Hall.

"You're in luck," said the young man at the ticket booth. "We only have two shows a day and the first one starts in ten minutes."

The auditorium was quickly filling up with cruise-ship passengers. The Four Rock Miners reunion party found seats in the second row.

At ten o'clock on the dot, an announcer came out to tell them the history of Skagway.

"The town didn't even exist until 1898," he began. "Some men found gold in the interior of Alaska, a part of the country along the Yukon River that also bordered Canada. When a ship carrying two tons of gold sailed into Seattle, word spread quickly."

"How much is a ton?" Benny whispered to Violet.

"A lot," she whispered back.

"Soon thousands of men and women were headed to Skagway, the closest port to the Klondike region by sea," the announcer said. "Boat fares in the summer of 1897 soared from two hundred dollars a person to a thousand dollars. By late summer, people were arriving daily on anything that floated. By fall, one hundred thousand people had landed in Skagway. They had to buy supplies for a year and hike to the goldfields, which were six hundred miles away."

Several people in the audience whistled at the distance.

The man continued his talk. "Many turned back when they saw the steep, dangerous passes they had to cross to reach the Yukon. But a lot of people *did* make it. When they came back, Skagway had grown into a rip-roaring town! There were plenty of places to spend money!"

Then dancers came onstage and danced to piano music.

When the show was over, the reunion party debated what to do next.

"I'm thirsty!" Benny declared. "I want a soda."

"Good idea," agreed Miss Parker. "All that listening made me thirsty, too."

The Sweet Tooth Saloon was their next stop.

Inside, Benny ordered a chocolate shake.

"It's funny," said Jessie, scooping ice cream with a long-handled spoon. "Even though it's kind of cold outside, I can still eat ice cream."

"I can eat ice cream *anytime*," Benny said. "Even in a blizzard!"

"Well, we won't have to worry about that," said Jennifer Wilson, laughing. "I doubt we'll see even a snowflake."

After their midmorning refreshments, no one wanted to eat lunch for a while. And when they did, the Pittmans quarreled about where they should go.

"Let's try the Prospector's Sourdough Restaurant," Grandfather suggested. "The prices are very reasonable, according to my guidebook."

"Hmmmpf," Mr. Pittman snorted. "Now I know why the old prospectors were so sour. They had to fork over a lot of dough for everything!"

Benny was confused. "What is he talking about?"

Violet answered as they went into the restaurant. "It's an expression, Benny. *Dough* is another word for 'money.' "

They all sat down in the restaurant, which was decorated with local artwork.

Jessie picked up her menu, but couldn't concentrate. Something Mr. Pittman had said earlier was bothering her.

One of us is a thief.

Suppose he's right, she thought. *Which one of us stole the scrapbook and raven?*

CHAPTER 4

Mystery Within a Mystery

Strolling along Broadway after lunch, the Aldens were warm enough to shed their coats and jackets.

Violet breathed in the clean, fresh air. The town was surrounded by the Skagway River, the bay, and the mountains. Ahead of her, Monique stopped at a store.

"I want to go shopping," she whined to her father. "We haven't bought anything since we got here."

"At these prices?" Mr. Pittman cried. "Look at how much those things in the window are!"

Miss Parker was consulting her guide-book. "This is a special shop. It's the oldest curio store in Alaska. Let's go in."

Benny tilted his head back to see the sign. "What's it called?"

"Kirmse's," said Grandfather as they all went inside. "Say, '*Kirm-zees.*' It might be Russian. Alaska was claimed by Russians way back in the 1700s. Of course, the Native Americans were already here. The United States bought Alaska from Russia in 1867. People thought Secretary of State William Seward was crazy for buying so much land so far north."

"They called his purchase 'Seward's Folly,' " Miss Parker added.

"What does *folly* mean?" asked Violet.

"A *folly* means 'a foolish mistake,' usually costing a lot of money," Grandfather answered. "But people soon changed their minds when they learned about Alaska's tremendous resources."

Monique patted back a huge fake yawn. "Please, no more history lessons!"

"Look at this," said Jennifer Wilson. She

was peering into a case that displayed items not for sale. "That's so beautiful."

Jessie leaned over to get a peek. "What a pretty necklace," she commented, admiring the dainty chain of the world's tiniest pure gold nuggets.

"I'd love to have that," Jennifer said with a sigh.

"No, here's the one we need," her husband said. He pointed to a watch chain made from the largest nuggets. "This chain is the heaviest and most valuable in the world, it says. If we sold that, we could buy a house and all the furniture we want!"

After glancing over the lovely items in the store, the group left.

"When are we going to do something *fun*?" complained Mark.

"This *is* fun," said Miss Parker. "I'm having a great time just seeing the town. Aren't you? Skagway is nothing like Sheboygan, Wisconsin, where I live."

"It's not like Greenfield, Connecticut, either," agreed Grandfather. "But in answer

to your question, Mark, tomorrow we're going gold hunting —"

"Yippee!" Benny cried.

"— then we'll take a few trips out of town. The four days will be over before you know it," Grandfather said.

"Not soon enough for me," Monique muttered.

But Jessie heard her. She couldn't understand why the older girl seemed so determined not to have a good time. Her brother was the same way.

Walking back to the Totem Lodge, the Alden children stayed together.

"You notice something?" Henry asked his brother and sisters.

"What?" said Benny.

"All anyone talks about here is money," Henry said. "Gold and money."

"Henry's right," said Jessie. "I think the town is neat, but everybody seems mostly interested in the gold part."

Violet tied the sleeves of her light jacket around her waist so she wouldn't have to carry it. "Maybe the theft of Grandfather's scrapbook and raven has something to do with money."

"Good point," Jessie said. "The thief could have taken those things to sell." Then she paused. "But the scrapbook isn't really worth anything, is it? It's just old photos."

"And those raven statues are everywhere," Benny put in. "Look, there's one in that window."

The raven he pointed to was bigger than the Four Rock Miners' statue, but the soapstone carving looked very similar, even down to the etched wing feathers.

"Miss Parker told us how important the raven is to Native American tribes," Jessie said. "So we can expect to see ravens all over the place."

"Then money wasn't the reason the thief took the scrapbook and statue?" reasoned Violet.

Henry shook his head. "I don't think we can rule out anything in this mystery. The strangest part is, how did anyone break into Grandfather's room while he was *in* it?"

"That," said Jessie, "is a mystery within a mystery."

Later, the Four Rock Miners reunion members met at the Northern Lights Pizzeria for dinner.

"Now, this is more like it," said Mrs. Pittman when they sat down and studied the menus.

"I love pizza," Benny said.

"You love *any* food," Violet said, laughing.

"Well — I'm not crazy about beets. Or brussels sprouts," Benny said seriously. Even the Pittmans laughed at that.

The restaurant was warm from the pizza ovens. Soon everyone was munching slices of pizzas topped with pepperoni, sausage, or mushrooms.

Mark bit into a piece, dragging the cheese way out. His sister giggled when the cheese string broke and stuck to his nose. For once, the Pittmans seemed to be enjoying themselves.

Mr. Pittman talked louder and louder, as

the place filled with other diners. "Let me tell you something, boy," he said to Steve Wilson, clapping him jovially on the back. "I'm going to *be* somebody someday. Mark my words, Wilson."

Miss Parker interrupted in her gentle voice. "You're special already, Earl. You have a fine family. There's no further need to prove yourself."

"Yes, there is," Mr. Pittman insisted, suddenly becoming surly. "And I'll do it, too!"

Violet, who sat across from Mark, watched him doodle on the napkin. Staring at the drawings upside down, she recognized birds with large heads and big beaks. Why was Mark drawing ravens?

Grandfather spoke up. "Well, I think my grandchildren are ready to call it a night. I know I am. We'll see you tomorrow morning at breakfast. Be ready for a big day!"

As they walked back to the Totem Lodge in the nippy air, Benny asked his grandfather, "Why is Mr. Pittman always so grumpy?"

"Oh, some people have trouble seeing

happiness, even when it's right in front of them," replied Grandfather.

"Well, his kids certainly aren't much fun," Henry put in. "All they do is mope and complain."

"I hope they won't be mopey when we go gold hunting," Jessie put in.

"Gold hunting is cool," said Benny. "How can anybody be mopey over *that*?"

Jessie kept her thoughts to herself. If there was a way to spoil the outing, Mark and Monique would find it.

Back at the lodge, Grandfather reported in at the front desk. Howie the bellhop was on night duty. He nodded to Grandfather and the children.

"Mr. Alden," said the evening desk clerk, "I've spoken to the maid who cleaned the third-floor rooms today. She didn't find a scrapbook or a raven statue under the beds or on the closet shelves."

"That's what I thought," Grandfather said with a sigh.

The clerk went on, "Of course, she isn't

permitted to go through the dressers or the guests' personal belongings."

"Of course," Grandfather agreed. "I'll speak to the rest of our group. Thank you for your help."

As they walked up to the third floor, Henry asked, "Are you going to ask the others to look in their luggage?"

"I hate to do it," Grandfather said. "It automatically assumes that one of us is a thief. Miss Parker and I both believe it's too soon to invade people's privacy. We'd have to bring the bags in one room and go through them with the others watching. To do that, we'd need everyone's agreement."

Jessie could imagine the fuss the Pittmans would make. "Do you think the scrapbook and raven will turn up before we leave?" she asked.

"I'm hoping that will happen," said Grandfather. "If you children want to stay up and read or talk, go ahead. I'll see you in the morning."

After saying good night to their grandfather, the Aldens gathered in Violet and Jessie's room to discuss the case.

"Suppose one of the others *did* steal the scrapbook and raven," Henry proposed. "What good will it do? Sooner or later, everyone gets a turn to keep the items. Why steal them out of turn?"

"Unless there's something we're over-looking," said Jessie. "Maybe the person who took the scrapbook and raven isn't re-ally interested in those old things, but in-stead is trying to get back at Grandfather."

"For what?" asked Benny. "Everybody loves Grandfather."

Violet smiled. "Not everyone knows Grandfather the way we do. Remember, the other people here have never met him be-fore this trip."

"I've been thinking about Mr. Pittman," Jessie said. "Remember how he told Steve he would be somebody someday? Suppose he took Grandfather's things to be famous."

"How would that make him famous?" Benny asked.

Jessie opened her mouth to comment, but

just then there was a knock at the door.

She slid off the bed to answer it.

Miss Parker stood in the doorway. Quickly glancing up and down the hallway, she whispered, "May I come in?"

"Sure." Jessie held the door open for the former teacher.

Miss Parker's face was flushed, as if she'd been running.

"Are you okay?" Violet asked.

"I'm fine, thanks," the older woman replied. "I've just been talking to your grandfather. I still feel terrible that the scrapbook and raven were stolen. Your grandfather told me you children are very good detectives and have solved a number of mysteries."

"That's true," stated Benny.

"But this case is tough," admitted Jessie.

Miss Parker pulled something from her gray tote bag. "I believe I have something that might help. I should have shown it to you sooner!"

CHAPTER 5

Miss Parker's Clue

The older lady sat down on the bed, and the children settled around her. From a side pocket of her tote, she pulled out an old envelope.

"I found this while I was going through my great-uncle's belongings," Miss Parker explained. "One of my Blake cousins sent me boxes of his things. She didn't want them cluttering up her apartment."

"What was in the boxes?" asked Benny.

"Nothing of great value," the teacher replied. "Things of sentimental value, but not worth much money. But this was interesting."

She opened the worn envelope.

Violet leaned forward. She could barely read the fine, spidery writing. It was addressed to Edward James Alden in Greenfield, Connecticut. A faint postmark was stamped April 16, 1910. The letter had been mailed to her ancestor!

"That was sent to Grandfather's great-uncle," she said.

"Yes, it was," said Miss Parker. She pulled out several sheets of tissue-thin paper filled with the same spidery handwriting. "I won't read you all of the letter because people in those days took a long time to get to the point. Basically it says my great-uncle couldn't make it to the annual Four Rock Miners reunion in Skagway."

"Why not?" Henry asked. "I thought it was a tradition."

"It was, but Uncle Pete's little daughter was very ill. He couldn't leave his family. It was a long trip from Wisconsin to Alaska and he didn't have the money, either."

"So what happened that year?" Jessie asked with interest. "Did they go?" This was a new twist. She thought the miners always met in Skagway, no matter what.

"The other three did," Miss Parker replied, carefully refolding the letter and slipping it back into the envelope. She tucked the envelope into the outside pocket of her bag.

"And your great-uncle didn't go?" asked Violet.

"Yes, Pete Blake stayed in Wisconsin. But you see, he had to pass the scrapbook and raven on to Harold Bell that year. So Pete asked Edward Alden what to do — mail the scrapbook and raven to Harold so he would have it for the reunion, or what?"

"Did they have mail back in those days?" asked Benny.

That broke them all up.

"Yes," said Miss Parker, wiping her eyes. "And it was after the Pony Express! Anyway, the other three men wrote to one another and decided to let Pete keep the scrapbook and raven for another year, for luck. Since money was tight and his daughter was sick, maybe having those things would help."

"And did it?" Jessie wanted to know.

Miss Parker shrugged. "Well, my uncle's daughter *did* get well and he got another job later that year. Who knows? I'm not a superstitious person, but back then a lot of people were. In fact, some people still won't walk under ladders or let a black cat cross their path."

"I'm super — whatever you said," Benny put in. "I never walk under ladders."

Everyone laughed again.

Miss Parker continued, "A new tradition was started. If any of the miners was having trouble of some sort, he was allowed to keep the scrapbook and statue an extra year. Or he could receive them out of turn to 'change his luck.' "

"Grandfather didn't know this?" asked Henry. Grandfather was the only member of the reunion group who had been attending the reunions for many years.

Miss Parker shook her head. "He had never heard of this tradition. No one knew about it until I found the letter. That's why I brought it with me. When the original miners died, this part of the reunion remained a secret."

Henry looked at Jessie. Jessie nodded back. She was thinking what he was thinking. Maybe the scrapbook and raven weren't worth money, but they might be valuable as good-luck charms. But who else knew about the letter?

Miss Parker sighed. "I feel so bad those things were stolen from your grandfather. They had been in my care, so in a way, I feel responsible —"

Just then Violet heard something outside, a slight shuffling sound. Was someone listening through the door?

"Keep talking," she whispered, sliding off the bed.

The others continued a general conversation as she crept over to the door.

Violet turned the handle silently and peered through the crack. She didn't see anyone. Opening the door wider, she looked down the hall. Was the door to room 309 closing? Or was it her imagination? The corridor wasn't very well lit.

She went back into the room.

"Anybody?" queried Henry.

Violet shook her head. "But I thought for *sure* I heard something out there."

"I should let you children get to bed," said Miss Parker. "It's late. See you in the morning."

Later, when the boys were across the hall in their room, Jessie asked Violet more about what she had heard.

"It sounded like shoes shuffling on a rug," she explained. "But I didn't see anybody. Except . . ."

"Except what?"

"Well, I thought I saw the door to room 309 closing when I looked down the hall," Violet said with a yawn.

Jessie said, "That's the Wilsons' room."

"I know," said Violet. "I suppose Steve or Jennifer could have been out filling their ice bucket."

A few minutes later, Jessie realized that Violet was wrong. "Getting ice is the bellhop's job," Jessie said. "Anyway, Steve and Jennifer are too nice to listen at doors."

Violet didn't reply. She was fast asleep.

Jessie stared at the ceiling, trying to sort her thoughts. But she was too tired to think about the mystery anymore. The Wilsons weren't the type to listen at doors. Were they?

Soon she was asleep herself.

Early the next morning, the Alden children went downstairs to breakfast. They located a table in the back where they could review the mystery in private.

"Miss Parker's letter is definitely a clue," Henry declared. "We must keep it a secret between Miss Parker, Grandfather, and us."

"Someone else might know about it. I'm pretty sure someone was listening to us last night," Violet said. Then she told the boys how she had seen the door to the Wilsons' room slowly closing. "But they're too nice to spy," she added.

"They are nice," Henry agreed. "But we can't let that fool us. Remember yesterday, when they were talking about selling the nugget watch chain to buy a house and furniture?"

"That was just talk," Violet said.

"Well, *someone* took Grandfather's scrapbook and statue. We shouldn't trust anyone," Henry said.

"Not even Miss Parker?" asked Benny. He liked her a lot.

Jessie tugged at her ponytail. "I think Henry's right. We really can't trust anyone. Suppose Miss Parker is in trouble and she needed to keep the scrapbook and raven another year, for luck."

"Why wouldn't she just tell the others about the letter at the reunion dinner and ask to keep them?" Violet reasoned. "Or at least tell Grandfather. I'm sure he'd let her have them another year."

"Stealing from Grandfather seems like a lot of trouble," Henry said. "Violet's right. Miss Parker doesn't seem like the sneaky type."

"Okay, let's rule out Miss Parker," Jessie said, relieved.

Before they could name any other suspects, the rest of the reunion party joined them.

"All set for a big day?" Grandfather asked the children, signaling the waiter for a pot of coffee. "We're going to pan for gold!"

"I hope I find lots of gold," Benny said eagerly. He jumped up from the table. "Let's go!"

Grandfather laughed. "Wait a second, Benny! We haven't even had breakfast yet!"

Miss Parker joined them, giving the Aldens a knowing wink. Jessie figured the older woman was glad they were on the case.

The Wilsons claimed the table next to them. Jennifer was as cheerful as always. Today she wore a pastel yellow sweater with geese stitched on the front. Her dark hair was held back with a yellow headband. Steve wore a plaid red-and-black shirt.

"I've decided to dress like the miners," he joked.

The Pittmans were late, as usual. They came into the dining room squabbling over who had gotten the least amount of sleep the night before.

"That mattress is a killer," grumbled Mrs. Pittman. "I'd be better off sleeping on the floor, except it's so cold."

"I wish I had my pillow from home," Monique griped, drooping in her seat.

After they had all ordered, Grandfather told them about the day's activity plan.

"We're walking down to the Skagway River," he announced. "The cruise ships dock there, so we can look at those."

"Who wants to look at a bunch of dumb old boats?" said Mark Pittman sourly.

Ignoring the teen's remark, Grandfather went on. "Then we'll head for the beach and let the young people pan for gold. The oldsters can pan, too," he added with a chuckle.

"How long is this trip going to take?" asked Mr. Pittman.

"We'll be gone the better part of the day," Grandfather replied. "I've already arranged for the hotel to fix us box lunches.

That way we won't have to run back into town and find a restaurant."

Mrs. Pittman nodded. "At least box lunches are cheaper."

"I hope I don't get a peanut butter sandwich," said Monique, wrinkling her nose. "Or yucky old bologna."

"I'll take yours!" Benny offered. He loved both peanut butter and bologna.

Grandfather cleared his throat. "I'm sure the hotel will fix nice lunches. As Benny suggested, we can always trade with one another."

Monique and Mark rolled their eyes at each other, bored before they had even begun the day. Violet hoped the teenagers wouldn't spoil Benny's fun. Her little brother was so excited about panning for gold.

When breakfast was over, the group met outside the dining room.

The hotel clerk was looking around the lobby. A cart with white rectangular boxes and small backpacks waited by the desk.

"Howie?" the clerk called. "Where is that boy?"

Benny saw where Howie was. The bell-hop was hiding behind the totem pole with the raven carved on it. The young man had been listening to the reunion group's plans.

Why was the bellhop so nosy?

CHAPTER 6

Panning for Gold

The desk clerk finally noticed Howie standing behind the totem pole. He called the bellhop over.

"You should have packed these lunches into those backpacks by now," the clerk scolded. "Do it quickly. We don't want to delay this party."

In no time, Howie slid a white box into each of the nylon packs and distributed one to each of the reunion members.

"Mine is red," Benny remarked.

"So is mine," said Miss Parker, slipping

the straps over her shoulders. "Our packs will be easy to spot."

The group left the lobby and walked down Broadway. It was warmer today. Soon everyone had peeled off the extra jacket or sweater.

"Here's a hardware store," Grandfather said, stopping at a building.

"Why are we going into a stupid old hardware store?" grumbled Monique.

"To buy pans," answered Grandfather. "You want to pan for gold, don't you?"

"It sounds like work," Monique said, blocking the doorway.

Miss Parker took the girl's hand and led her into the store so the rest could enter. "Don't be silly, Monique. It'll be fun! Who knows what we'll find?"

Grandfather picked out four round tin pans for the Aldens and a small, inexpensive shovel.

Mr. Pittman said, "I suppose I have to fork over good money on tools for my kids, too. Something they'll use once."

"I'll purchase all the pans," Grandfather said generously, adding two more to the pile on the counter. "We'll share the shovel."

At the last minute, Steve bought a pan for himself and Jennifer. "Maybe we'll get lucky!" he said.

Get lucky. Jessie thought about Steve's words as they walked down to the harbor. Violet thought she'd seen the Wilsons' door closing last night. The Wilsons were newlyweds; they didn't have much money. Could they have stolen the scrapbook and raven statue to bring them luck?

Two huge cruise ships were moored in the harbor. One was called the *Sea Star,* the other *Princess of the Waves.* The ships were enormous.

"I want a boat like that when I grow up!" Benny exclaimed.

"How are you going to sail it?" asked Henry, smiling.

"I think you need a big crew to help you run such a big boat. Don't you remember that cruise we took?" Violet asked.

"You've been on a cruise?" Edie Pittman asked sharply.

"Yes," said Jessie. "Grandfather took us. We had a great time."

"Okay, we've seen the ships. Big deal. When are we going to get this show on the road?" asked Mark.

The coastline curved inland where the cruise ships were anchored in deep water, then jutted out again. That was where the daily ferry docked. The group followed a long spit of land. Gulls shrieked overhead, sometimes dipping low.

At last the reunion party reached the beach where they were permitted to pan for gold. A guide who worked there explained the rules.

"While you're with me, you may pan as long as you like," he said. "And you may keep whatever gold you find."

The reunion party members weren't the only tourists on the beach. Other tour groups were trying their luck as well.

Violet got her pan out of her pack. "Okay, Grandfather. How do we do this?"

James Alden pulled the shovel from the strap in his own pack. "There's a trick to it. I want everyone to watch."

The reunion group gathered around as he shoveled a scoop of gravel from the water's edge. Then he added a scoop of water to the gravel in the pan. Squatting, he swirled the water in the pan.

Then he carefully poured off the gravel and water, frowning at the silt remaining in the bottom of the pan.

"Nothing," he pronounced. "Not a grain of gold. But that's how you do it. Swirl the water in the pan, but not too fast. Gold is heavier than water, but you don't want to dump it out with the other rocks and sand."

"Let me try!" Benny said eagerly. Taking the shovel, he filled his pan.

"Not too much," Grandfather instructed, dumping out the excess. "You have to be able to swirl the water."

Soon everyone had a turn at the shovel and was busy swirling his or her pan.

"This isn't easy," Jessie remarked. "I keep tipping my pan over!"

"Imagine doing this all day long, day after day," said Miss Parker. "That's what many of the old miners did."

Violet emptied her pan. "What does the gold *look* like?"

"Bright, shiny, and yellow," Miss Parker answered. "It can be tiny flecks or a nice big nugget."

"Well, those old-timers certainly didn't get rich doing this," Mark said, filling his pan for the third time.

Grandfather nodded. "You're right, Mark. Panning wasn't the most effective way to find gold. Besides panning, miners also used the rocker method."

"What's that?" asked Benny. He pictured the rocking chair back home.

"The rocker was a special device," Grandfather replied. "Miners built a box on a curved base. On top of the box was a wire screen. Stones bigger than half an inch couldn't go through it. One miner shoveled gravel on the screen, then rocked the box as another man added water to wash stones through. Below the screen was a piece of cloth. Smaller gold nuggets would drop on this cloth and they could pick them up."

"That sounds like hard work, too," remarked Henry.

"It was," said Miss Parker. "People thought when they got here they could simply pick gold nuggets out of the creek beds. They found out otherwise."

Benny was swirling very carefully. He wanted to be the first to find gold! But every time he poured off the water and rocks, there were no bright yellow flecks on the bottom.

"Hey!" squealed Monique. "I think I found some!"

Everyone crowded around as Monique held out her pan. In the saucerlike bottom were tiny bits of bright stones.

"Congratulations," Grandfather declared. "You have definitely struck gold!"

"Oh, my gosh!" Monique danced around. "What should I do with it? Is it mine to keep?"

"It ought to be, given the cost of this trip," said Mr. Pittman. He offered Monique his handkerchief. "Here, put the stones in this."

"As the guide said, any and all gold you find is yours," Grandfather told her. He helped Monique tie a knot in the corner of the handkerchief so the grains wouldn't fall out.

"I can't believe it!" Monique was still saying. "I found gold!"

Jessie was amazed that something had excited the other girl. For once Monique wasn't acting bored and mopey.

But her brother jeered, "Don't go bananas over those itty-bitty little specks."

"You're just jealous because *you* haven't found any!" Monique retorted.

Suddenly Violet felt sorry for Monique. Her brother wasn't acting nice at all. "Monique, did you swirl your pan a certain way?" she asked the other girl. "Maybe we've been doing it wrong."

"Well —" Monique began.

But Mark tossed his pan down. "Oh, this is for babies."

"*I'm* not a baby," Benny said. He wished

he had been the first to find gold, but he was glad for Monique. Now he was determined to be the *second* one to find gold.

The kids spread out down the beach while the grown-ups found a sunny spot to have lunch. Benny had to be called twice before he quit panning long enough to eat.

When it was time to go back to the hotel, Benny still hadn't found a single grain of gold.

His shoulders bowed, he stowed his pan in his pack.

Henry was about to go cheer up his brother, but Monique reached Benny first. She offered the knotted handkerchief to him.

"You deserve this," she said. "You've worked harder than any of us today. I bet you shoveled a hundred times!"

Benny's eyes were round. "You mean it? I can keep your gold?"

"As a present from me," said Monique.

"Are you sure you want to give it away?" Henry asked.

She shrugged. "It's mine. I can give it away."

Benny ran ahead to show Grandfather.

Henry walked alongside Monique. "That was very nice. Benny will never forget it."

"He's a cute kid. You're all nice. I know my family can be a pain sometimes —" She stopped, smiling. "I was hoping we could be friends."

"Well . . . sure," Henry replied. Monique chatted all the way back to the hotel, but Henry was suspicious. Why the sudden change? Was Monique friendly because she wondered what the Aldens knew about the theft?

What was even more odd, he decided, was that Monique and Mark never once said anything about the theft of the scrapbook and raven statue. Did that mean *they* were the thieves?

It had been a long day, Jessie thought. That afternoon the group did more sight-seeing, then had dinner at the Dockside Restaurant.

It was fun eating and watching the cruise ships leave, all lit up like Christmas trees.

But she was glad when they were finally back at the lodge for the evening.

After Grandfather fetched their keys at the front desk, the children said good night and walked up to the third floor.

Jessie put the key in the lock and turned it. As she pushed open the door, she had a strange feeling.

"What is it?" Violet asked, switching on the lamp.

Jessie stood perfectly still. The room looked just as it had when they had been there earlier. The housekeeper had made the twin beds and vacuumed the rug. But something was different. . . .

Then she noticed what was wrong. She and Violet kept their hair ribbons and barrettes in two piles on the dresser. The piles had been moved. Not much, but pushed aside. It was as if someone had been in a hurry, looking for something.

"Someone has searched our room," Jessie declared.

From across the hall, Henry and Benny

bounded over. "Look what we found!" Benny cried.

Henry held out a folded sheet of hotel stationery. In printed letters were the words:

GO HOME IF YOU KNOW WHAT'S GOOD FOR YOU!

CHAPTER 7

The Missing Scrapbook

Jessie stared at the note. "Something really weird is going on here," she said. "You guys better come inside."

Henry and Benny went into the girls' room. Benny still carried the knotted handkerchief Monique Pittman had given him.

"The stuff on our dresser has been moved," Violet told the boys. "Jessie spotted it first. We usually keep our hair ribbons in two piles by the lamp."

Benny nodded. "They look kind of messy now."

"Exactly," Jessie said. "Like someone brushed them aside —"

"While he or she was searching the dresser drawer," Henry finished. "Looking for what, I wonder?"

Jessie shook her head. "And now this note! What does it mean?"

"Someone wants us out of here," Benny said soberly.

"They also want something we have," Violet added. "But *what*? How can anybody think we have the scrapbook or raven? Why would we take it from Grandfather? That would be silly."

Henry thought about the night before. "Wait a minute! Violet, you heard someone outside this door last night when Miss Parker was here."

"When she was talking about that old letter —" Violet clapped a hand over her mouth. "Do you think the person who listened came back today to take the letter?"

"But it belonged to Miss Parker," Jessie said with a frown. "She took it back with her. I saw her put the envelope in her tote bag. So that doesn't make sense."

"Unless," Benny said, "the person who listened didn't hear everything. Maybe he only heard *part* of what we were talking about."

"Good point," Henry said, nodding. "What is it Grandfather says? 'Eavesdroppers seldom profit.' "

"What does *that* mean?" asked Benny.

"It means eavesdroppers can't often use the information they overhear. It doesn't do them any good," Jessie replied. "Okay, we have someone who wants Miss Parker's letter. Only he thinks it belongs to us, so he searched our room for it. When he didn't find it, he got mad and put a note under your door. Why not *our* door?"

Violet was studying Henry's note. She knew that handwriting. . . .

"Mark wrote this," she blurted.

"Are you sure?" Henry asked.

"Remember last night when his dad was talking about being somebody? Mark began doodling on his paper napkin," she answered. "He wrote his name, then drew ravens."

Henry tapped the note. "If Mark wrote the note, then maybe he's the guy who broke into your room."

"And maybe the same one who stole the scrapbook and statue," Jessie concluded. But the pieces didn't fit. "Why would he do that? And why tell us to get out of town?"

"As a joke?" Violet suggested. "I've tried to like those two, but it's hard."

Benny held up his handkerchief. "But Monique gave me her gold! I think she wants to be friends."

"That's what she said," Henry said. "Still, I have a funny feeling about her and Mark. I think they might have another motive." Henry put the note in his shirt pocket. "Well, we're not going to solve this mystery tonight. Tomorrow everybody needs to be extra alert. Remember, we can't trust anybody yet."

No matter how nice they seem, he thought as he led his little brother across the hall to their room.

*   *   *

"What do we have to do today, James?" grumbled Mr. Pittman over juice and scrambled eggs the next morning. Even a hearty breakfast couldn't put him in a good mood.

Miss Parker rose to Grandfather's defense. "We should be grateful. James has saved us the trouble of planning. He's helped us make the most of this trip."

Across the table, Mark rolled his eyes. "Yeah, right," he mumbled.

Henry was watching him closely. He believed Mark Pittman might be the key to the mystery.

"Actually, we're going on a train ride today," said Grandfather.

"Oh, boy!" Benny exclaimed. He loved trains as much as big boats.

"This will be an all-day excursion," Grandfather went on. "We'll see some of the countryside the miners had to hike through to get to the goldfields."

"Is there a food car on the train?" Benny wanted to know.

Grandfather laughed. "No, this is a small steam train without a dining car. The hotel is packing lunches again."

Edie Pittman was touching up her lipstick. "I hope they give us better food than last time."

"I'm sure the staff will be happy to fix you a different lunch," Grandfather told her. "They're used to accommodating special diets. In fact, there's the bellhop now, with the cart. You can request whatever you like."

The white boxes were already packed in the nylon backpacks, but Howie was happy to take one back to the kitchen and have a special lunch fixed for Mrs. Pittman.

The grown-ups waited in the lobby with their packs while Mrs. Pittman's lunch was being prepared. Mark and Monique disappeared upstairs to their room.

The Alden children found Miss Parker alone.

"How's the case coming?" she asked.

"We're stuck," Jessie confessed. "We need to know if you still have that letter you showed us."

The teacher picked up the gray tote she used as a purse. "It's in —" Her mouth formed an O of surprise as she checked the side pocket. "It's gone! My letter is gone!"

"Are you sure it's not in your room?" asked Jessie.

"Yes," the older woman replied. "After all that's happened, I keep the letter with me. At least I thought I did."

The children looked at one another. This was getting serious. The thief had succeeded in stealing Miss Parker's letter. What would the thief take next?

At last the group was ready to leave. They walked down Broadway, turning on Second Street. The weather was gorgeous — sunny, with cloudless blue skies.

The White Pass and Yukon Rail Depot was also the information center for the Klondike Gold Rush National Historical Park. While Grandfather and the other adults purchased tickets, the children wandered around the exhibits. Old photos of sourdoughs and prospecting tools were displayed on the walls and in cases. Then they went back outside.

Soon a steam engine puffed down the tracks.

Benny jumped up and down with excitement. "What a cool train!"

"Yes," agreed Steve Wilson. "Those old steam trains aren't anything like modern ones." He looked excited himself.

Jennifer giggled when Steve yelled like a conductor, "All abooooarrd!"

"Pretty good!" said the real conductor. "Step aboard, folks. We're about to take a trip back in time."

"I hope I don't get sick," Benny said.

Jessie laughed as she followed her brother onto the train. "This won't be like a ride at an amusement park," she said as they sat down.

Grandfather sat across from them, letting Violet have the window. "He means we're going to travel the same path the old-timers did. We have the train to ourselves today."

Henry wound up sitting with Monique. Mark found a seat by himself across from them. For once, neither of the Pittman teenagers looked bored. In fact, Henry noticed an excited sparkle in their eyes.

The engine puffed a huge cloud of steam, tooted mightily, then rolled down the tracks.

"The trip is almost twenty-one miles long," the conductor said. "This is the very same countryside the old miners walked, carrying on their backs enough supplies to last for a year. Notice the rugged terrain. It hasn't changed a bit."

The conductor pointed out parts of the original White Pass Trail. Rusted pans and other gear still lay where miners had dropped extra supplies to lighten their load.

The train wound along the mountain, under tunnels, and over a trestle. The deep gulch below made the passengers gasp.

"Wasn't it hard for the prospectors to get over that gulch?" asked Miss Parker.

"A lot of them didn't make it," said the conductor. "The White Pass caused many to turn back."

At the summit, the train stopped and everyone got off, taking their packs.

Jessie, who had sat with Benny, went back onboard to get his sweater. It was chilly on the summit. She saw Monique dawdling down the aisle behind her.

"I love eating outdoors," Jessie commented.

"I hate it," Monique said. "The wind blows everything around. It's so messy."

Well, I tried, Jessie thought. Apparently nothing pleased the older girl. Whatever excitement Monique had shown at the beginning of the trip had disappeared.

As they ate, the conductor told them more about the hardships the miners faced. The walk to the goldfields along the Yukon River was six hundred miles. They had to get there before the long winter and build a shelter. Then they waited until spring before they could even start digging for gold.

All too soon, it was time to reboard the train.

Violet walked ahead of Grandfather so she could sit by the window again. And then she saw it.

The scrapbook was lying on Grandfather's seat.

"Look!" she cried. "The missing scrap-book!"

Grandfather picked it up in amazement. "How did that get here?"

Everyone peppered everyone else with questions. No one knew anything. Violet was as amazed as the others. Someone had deliberately brought the scrapbook with them on the trip. And given it back.

But why?

Who would do such a strange thing?

Jessie looked at Monique, sitting with Henry. Monique had been the last to get off the train. There was enough room in the packs to stash the scrapbook. And Monique had had enough time to take it out and lay it on Grandfather's seat.

Then there was Mark's note. Was this just a prank between two bored teenagers?

Tomorrow was their last day in Skagway. Only one more day to track down the raven and find out the truth.

CHAPTER 8

Great-uncle Edward's Message

"Well, it certainly looks like the scrapbook and raven were stolen by someone in our group," said Miss Parker as she ate her salad. "And my uncle Pete's letter. But why on earth?"

Grandfather shook his head wearily. "Who knows?"

The reunion party had decided to split up for dinner. The Pittmans chose the pizzeria and the Wilsons wanted to dine alone at the Golden North. "To get away from those awful Pittmans," Jennifer confessed earlier to Jessie.

The Aldens chose to eat at the Totem Lodge. Grandfather asked Miss Parker to join them. After discussing the train trip, everyone soon began talking about the mystery.

Grandfather had brought the scrapbook with him. "I'm not letting it out of my sight," he said, setting the book by his plate.

"Can I see it?" Violet asked. "I never really had a chance to look at it."

"Certainly." He passed the leather-bound book to her.

Jessie, Benny, and Henry leaned closer as Violet slowly turned the heavy paper pages. Black triangles attached each corner of the photos to the pages. Captions beneath the pictures were written in white ink.

"Uncle Edward sure had fancy handwriting," Benny remarked, trying to read the curlicued script.

"It's like drawing," said Violet, admiring a capital *A* that seemed to enclose a bird's nest in its loops.

"That's probably where you get your artist's talent, Violet," Henry said.

"Yeah," agreed Benny. "From Great-great-great —" He lost track of the "greats."

"Just say Uncle Edward," Jessie said with a giggle.

The black-and-white photos showed the four miners standing in front of buildings the kids recognized in Skagway. "Only there aren't any cars," Benny pointed out. "Just horses." Later photographs showed the men, who'd all grown beards, posed in front of their claim. Four stacked rocks were distinct in the foreground.

Jessie nudged Henry. "Look who just came in."

Henry didn't need Jessie to tell him. He could hear the Pittmans before they entered the dining room. Monique and Mark glanced at the Aldens as they followed their parents to a table across the room.

Howie, who was on duty as busboy that evening, filled the Pittmans' water glasses.

Miss Parker commented, "I'm surprised to see them here. I wonder what happened at the pizzeria?"

"Maybe they ran out of pizza," said Benny.

James Alden laughed. "If I were the owner of that restaurant, I think I'd conveniently run out of pizza, too! Those people can be quite trying."

"That's putting it mildly," Miss Parker said, smiling. "At least they are well away from us."

Jessie took the scrapbook from Violet so she could see the pictures better. As she did, a loose photo fluttered to the floor.

Before Jessie could bend to pick it up, Howie leaped across the room and scooped up the photo. At the same time, Monique stood up and collided with Howie.

"Very sorry, miss," Howie apologized.

"It's okay," Monique said, giving him a dazzling smile.

Jessie was astonished. Was this the same girl who complained about every single

thing? Then she noticed that Monique was staring at the back of the photo. So was Howie.

"Thanks for getting that for me," Jessie told Howie, plucking the photo from his fingers.

He gazed hard at the picture, then said, "Anytime."

Monique went out through the doors shaped like totem poles without a word to Jessie.

"What was that all about?" asked Violet.

"I'm not sure," said Jessie. "But I bet it has to do with this picture."

The photo showed the men together in town. The two in the center, Edward Alden and Harold Bell, were both holding the raven statue, as if one were trying to take it from the other. The miners were all grinning. On the back, in Edward Alden's flowing script, was written, *"Wrestling for the raven."*

"It's just two guys messing around," said Benny.

Henry looked at Howie, who was busily

clearing a table. "Maybe. The picture sure seemed to catch Howie's and Monique's eyes."

"Are there captions written on the backs of the other photos?" Violet asked Jessie.

Carefully Jessie pried a few pictures from their triangular corners. "No," she pronounced. "Just that one."

"I think it's a message from Uncle Edward," said James Alden.

Miss Parker agreed. "A clue from the past. But what does it mean? We don't have the raven anymore."

"We must get it back tomorrow," said Violet. "If we find the raven, I think this whole mystery will be solved!"

But would they have enough time? she wondered. Could they solve a baffling case with only one more day in Alaska?

"The guide is here!" cried Benny. He had been waiting just outside the dining room near the totem pole with the raven carved on it.

On their last full day, the reunion group

was going to hike into the countryside. Grandfather came out of the dining room to shake hands with a young blond man wearing hiking boots and khaki pants with many pockets and flaps.

"You must be Gil," said Grandfather. "I'm James Alden. We're all looking forward to seeing the country on foot."

"What kind of pants are those?" said Benny admiringly.

"Cargo pants," replied Gil with a friendly smile. "You must be Benny. They probably make these pants in your size."

Just then the others filed into the lobby. Gil was introduced to the rest of the reunion party.

Howie wheeled in the cart with the day packs. When he saw the guide, he ducked his head and quickly distributed the packs, without saying a word.

Benny made sure he got a red one. His pack contained the white box lunch, a bottle of water, and a tiny first-aid kit. He wondered why Howie was suddenly so shy around them.

Everyone knew about the last-day hike. Jessie had made sure the Aldens had on comfortable walking shoes and extra sweaters. But Mrs. Pittman had come downstairs wearing high-heeled sandals and a dressy skirt. Jessie bet the woman's feet would hurt before they had walked far.

"We're going to take the Chilkoot Pass," Gil explained. "That's the trail the earliest sourdoughs took to the goldfields. You've heard it's six hundred miles long. We'll only walk about three miles each way. Everybody ready?"

Monique had been leaning against the totem pole. With a huge sigh, she slouched after her brother.

The trail began just outside of town. Gil stopped to tell them a little more about it.

"Prospectors had to carry their supplies on this trail, including enough food to last a year. It took them about three months to reach the Yukon Territory, if they were lucky," Gil said. "Later, during the Gold Rush, the White Pass was discovered. That trail was longer, but less steep. It's the one the White Pass and Yukon Railroad is on."

"We rode that yesterday," Benny put in.

"Great!" said Gil. "Now you can see both trails."

Today it was cloudy and chilly. Jessie was glad to have that extra sweater. Monique and Mark walked by themselves, well away from the others. Jessie wondered what they were talking about. They were so deep in conversation, she knew they weren't listening to the guide.

"Getting to the goldfields was very difficult," Gil was saying. "If they didn't start early enough, they had to wait out the winters in Skagway. If they started too late, they'd be caught in heavy snows. And a simple mistake could sometimes be very dangerous."

"Like what?" asked Henry. His long legs easily kept up with Gil's stride.

"Like not changing their socks if they got wet," Gil replied. "Wet socks freeze and soon the person is sick."

"Were there any women on the trail?" Jessie asked.

"Oh, yes," Gil answered. "They worked in the towns and miners' camps. They ran hot baths and washed clothes and cooked. One woman earned fifty thousand dollars in seven years by baking apple pies and dough-nuts. A miner who'd been eating beans for months would pay almost anything for a good home-cooked meal."

"Beans?" Benny repeated. "All they ate was beans?"

"Beans, bacon, potatoes, and onions. That was the miner's diet. And sourdough bread, if he had flour." Gil grinned. "Still want to be a prospector?"

"Only if I can have ice cream," Benny said, making the others laugh.

A large black bird soared across the sky.

"That's a raven," said Gil.

Violet snapped pictures of the bird. "I thought a raven was like a crow," she said. "But it's so much bigger!"

"Ravens and crows are in the same bird family," Gil explained. "But as you can see, the raven is the largest. Ravens are very smart. They like to hide bright, shiny objects. And they can talk."

"Like parrots?" asked Benny, remembering a parrot on a recent trip to Florida.

"A parrot sounds like a bird talking," said Gil. "Ravens can sound like *people* when they speak."

By now the group had hiked until Skagway was just a speck behind them.

"We'll stop here," said Gil. "To rest and have lunch."

They all found a place to sit down and take off their packs.

"My pack weighs a ton!" Miss Parker said with a laugh. "I can't imagine carrying a year's worth of food for six hundred miles!"

"My feet are killing me." Edie Pittman kicked off her sandals and rubbed her swollen toes.

"I told you not to wear those shoes," her husband said as he rummaged in his pack for the bottle of water.

"We have first-aid kits in our packs," Grandfather said helpfully. "You should cover those blisters with Band-Aids, Mrs. Pittman."

"I *should* have stayed at the hotel," was her sour reply.

Gil quickly pointed to the distant mountain pass. "Back in the Gold Rush days, an endless line of men climbed the trail, one after the other, every day."

"We saw a picture of that," said Violet. "In one of the museums."

Next Gil showed them rusted objects along the side of the trail. "Those are things that were dropped or tossed away by the miners. Those items are now artifacts, protected by the Park Service. Please do not touch or take them, but you can take photographs."

Photograph. The word reminded Jessie of Uncle Edward's message on the back of the scrapbook picture. Why did he only write on that photo and none of the others?

Then she unzipped her pack and took out her box lunch and bottle of water.

"Good idea," said Miss Parker, who sat next to Jessie. She shifted her pack to her lap. "Honestly, it feels like a rock is in here!"

Jessie and Miss Parker stared at each other.

"The raven!" Jessie whispered.

Hurriedly, the teacher unzipped her red pack. "Oh, I certainly hope so! It makes sense — yesterday our mysterious thief returned the scrapbook. . . ."

She pulled out a rounded lump wrapped in newspaper. The Aldens gathered around as Miss Parker tore off the paper.

"A plain old rock!" Benny cried in dismay.

Miss Parker shoved the stone to the ground. "Yes, only a rock." She looked around at the reunion party. "Is this some kind of joke?"

If it was, Henry thought, *it wasn't very funny.*

CHAPTER 9

The Raven Speaks

James Alden stood. "Does anybody know anything about this? I'm sure the cook didn't put in a rock as part of her lunch."

Monique and Mark both snickered.

Even their father didn't think it was amusing. "Be quiet," he told them. "Can't you see Miss Parker is upset?"

The former teacher was on the verge of tears. "I thought for sure the raven had been returned. Who would do such a mean thing?"

"Yeah? Who?" asked Steve Wilson, gazing around the reunion group.

Jennifer put her arm around Miss Parker's shoulders. "I think it was just a silly stunt. I'm sure whoever did it is sorry."

Violet was glad Jennifer was trying to help Miss Parker feel better, but she wondered if the guilty person *was* sorry. Someone had deliberately wrapped up a stone shaped like the raven statue and placed it in Miss Parker's pack. It wasn't an accident.

Their guide was confused. "What's going on?" asked Gil.

Grandfather hastily explained about the Four Rock Miners' annual reunion and how the scrapbook and raven were passed along each year.

"Yes, we've heard about your group," said Gil, nodding. "The reunions are practically legendary."

"Well, this year our group will really be legendary," Grandfather said. "The scrapbook and statue were stolen right after the dinner ceremony. The scrapbook was returned yesterday on the train ride. And now we thought the raven was, too. But apparently this was just a joke."

No one except the Pittmans had eaten their lunch. Even Benny had only taken one bite from his sandwich.

Jessie urged him to eat more, but Benny shook his head. "I don't want to eat."

Jessie noticed the incident didn't hurt the Pittman family's appetite. They ate every crumb in the white boxes, leaving their trash on the ground.

Gil began picking up napkins and paper cups from the picnic site. "I hate to shorten your outing," he said, "but we'd better head back. I'm afraid it might rain."

"I don't know if my feet will stand it," groaned Mrs. Pittman, reluctantly slipping into her sandals.

Miss Parker walked beside Grandfather. Jessie and Henry walked behind them.

"I feel so bad," they heard Miss Parker tell Grandfather. "I really wanted the statue returned to you."

"We still have this evening," Grandfather said consolingly. "We may find it yet."

"Why don't we just ask everyone to open their suitcases?" Henry asked his grandfather. "We know someone in our group took those things."

Grandfather sighed. "Forcing people to open their bags violates their privacy. We'd need everyone to voluntarily cooperate and I doubt the Pittmans would go along with it."

"That's because they're the ones with something to hide," said Jessie.

"We don't know that," Grandfather cautioned. "Remember, Jessie, in this country everyone is innocent until proven guilty."

Even if they act guilty? she thought. But she knew Grandfather was right.

Back at the hotel, the desk clerk was surprised to see the reunion party walking dejectedly through the door.

"It hasn't started to rain yet, has it?" he inquired, his eyebrows raised.

Grandfather reassured the clerk. "We just decided to return a bit sooner."

With a ring of the desk bell, Howie rushed over with the luggage cart.

"I'll take your packs," he said, bending to pile the blue, green, and red backpacks as they were handed to him.

When Henry shrugged the straps off his shoulders and gave Howie his pack, he noticed a faded corner of paper sticking out of the bellhop's shirt pocket. It looked familiar. Then he realized what it was.

The missing letter!

What was Howie doing with Miss Parker's letter?

Henry went over to Jessie and Violet. "We need to talk. Where's Benny?"

"Over by the dining room totem pole," said Violet.

"He's probably hungry," Jessie remarked. "He barely ate any of his lunch."

"None of us did," said Henry. "But the totem pole is a good place to talk, away from the others."

When Benny saw them coming, he asked, "What's up?" He knew the look on Henry's face had to do with the mystery.

"I saw something in Howie's pocket,"

Henry reported. "A corner of an envelope —"

"Miss Parker's letter!" Benny guessed.

"It looked like it," said Henry. "But I can't figure out why Howie would have it. It should be Mark."

"Or Monique," Jessie put in. "Those two are our most likely suspects."

Violet shook her head. "I'm not so sure. Haven't you seen the way Howie's always around whenever we're making plans? I think he listens to everything that's going on."

"And maybe," Henry stated, "he listens at doors!"

Benny was trying to remember something. The first night in the hotel . . . he could picture Grandfather getting their room keys from the guy at the hotel desk. But the Pittmans had trouble. Later, when he was in bed, he heard Howie leading Steve and Jennifer Wilson down the hall. Jennifer was asking about the totem pole decorations.

"They're hollow!" Benny exclaimed.

The others stared at him.

"What's hollow?" asked Violet.

"These!" Benny thumped the totem pole. "I heard Howie talking to Steve and Jennifer in the hall the first night we were here. Jennifer asked him about the totem poles. Howie said real totem poles are made of solid wood. But these are hollow!"

He thumped it again. Sure enough, the wood echoed hollowly.

"And this one," Benny said, "has a raven carved on it."

Jessie nodded. "Now things are starting to make sense. The raven is important to the Native Americans who live in Alaska. They carve ravens on totem poles and make little statues like the one the Four Rock Miners bought."

"And Mark was doodling ravens on his napkin the other night," Violet reminded them. "Maybe he *is* mixed up in this."

Henry waggled his finger to make a point. "And who have we seen hiding behind this totem pole, eavesdropping on us?"

"Howie!" Jessie replied.

They tipped their necks back. The raven was just over Henry's head, carved between a bear and a seal.

"I know where Grandfather's raven is," said Benny confidently. "But I can't reach."

"I can." Standing tall, Henry rapped the raven carving. "It's hollow, all right."

Jessie held her breath as Henry poked and pulled at the carving. Suddenly the raven section swung outward. "Is anything in there?" she asked anxiously.

"Yes." On his tiptoes, Henry lifted out a round object wrapped in newspaper. He gave the package to Benny. "You figured it out, so you should open it."

Sinking to the carpet, Benny yanked at the wrappings. He knew this time it wouldn't be an ordinary rock. The Four Rock Miners' soapstone raven lay on his knees.

"Grandfather's raven," he said triumphantly.

A shadow fell across Benny's small figure.

He looked up to see Mark Pittman.

"So," jeered Mark, "looks like you found that ugly bird statue."

Henry stepped forward. He was about to ask if Mark had put the statue in the hiding place when Monique and the Wilsons walked over.

"You found it!" Jennifer cried. "How wonderful! Look, everybody! The Aldens found the missing statue!"

Grandfather, Miss Parker, and the older Pittmans rushed over.

"Oh, I'm so glad!" said Miss Parker. "Wherever did you find it?"

"In one of the totem poles," Benny explained. "It's hollow. Behind the part with the raven on it is a secret hiding place."

Miss Parker turned to Grandfather. "James, you were absolutely right! Your grandchildren are excellent detectives!"

Gil came over to see what the excitement was about.

"So this is the famous Four Rock Miners' soapstone statue," he said. "It's amazing to see such an early carving. May I examine it?"

Benny glanced at Grandfather. His grandfather nodded. Benny figured the raven couldn't be stolen again, not with everyone watching.

"Hmmm." Gil turned the statue over in his hands, then hefted it, as if checking its weight.

"Is something wrong?" asked Miss Parker.

"This is the same statue that has been passed down from generation to generation?" Gil inquired.

Miss Parker looked confused. "Why, yes. I mean, it's the one I received from my aunt. She used to attend the reunions but is unable to make the trip anymore, so she gave the scrapbook and raven to me."

Grandfather added, "I've seen this raven many times over the years. It's the same one. Something about this statue is obviously bothering you."

"Yes," replied Gil. "Since you are all present, would you mind if I performed a little experiment?"

"You're not going to hurt the statue, are you?" asked Miss Parker.

Edie Pittman flapped a hand. "Who could hurt anything that ugly?"

"I just want to nick the bottom," said Gil. "It won't show, I promise." From one of the many pockets of his cargo pants he took out a penknife. Turning the statue bottom side up, he carefully scraped. Black coating came off on the knife blade.

"What is it?" asked Henry.

"Just as I thought," said Gil. "Although this raven can't really talk, it spoke to me in its own way. The statue is too heavy to be soapstone. It's only covered with a substance that *looks* like soapstone."

"Well, if the raven isn't made of soapstone, then what is it carved from?" asked Violet.

Gil smiled slowly, holding up the scratched statue for them all to see the yellow gleam.

"Gold."

CHAPTER 10

Benny's Mystery Within a Mystery

At first everyone was too stunned to speak.

Then Benny said, "Gold!"

"Yes," said Gil, scratching away the imitation soapstone covering to reveal more of the yellow metal beneath. "The Four Rock Miners apparently found an enormous nugget, then had a Native American artist carve it into a raven and cover it with this blackish substance."

"But why would they do that?" asked Jessie. "Gold is beautiful. Why coat it with that dull black stuff?"

Gil carefully continued to scrape. "Probably to keep it a secret. Maybe one of them found the nugget. Rather than split it four ways, they decided to leave it in one piece, like a trophy. So they had it carved and then covered so no one would know it was gold."

Grandfather shook his head unbelievingly. "All these years, we've been passing a solid gold bird back and forth!"

"Yes," said Earl Pittman in a greedy tone. "And now it's your turn to have it, James Alden. What are you going to do with it?"

Miss Parker's eyes flashed. "Are you implying that James is going to sell the raven now that he knows it's gold? I think you should apologize, Mr. Pittman."

"Well, I —" Mr. Pittman turned a deep shade of red.

Henry noticed Mark and Monique edging away.

"Come back, you two!" he called.

"We're tired," Monique whined. "We want to go upstairs to our rooms."

"I think you'd better stay," Henry told them. "We have some questions for you guys. Like who put the scrapbook on Grandfather's seat on the train yesterday."

"Do we have to listen to these kids?" Mark complained to his mother.

His mother crossed her arms. "This whole trip has been fishy. I'd like some answers myself."

"Where is Howie?" Benny asked suddenly. He had figured out part of the mystery within a mystery.

The bellhop had been hanging around when they discovered the raven statue hidden in the totem pole. But now the young man had disappeared.

"I'll find him," said Steve. He went over to the hotel manager and told him the story.

Soon Steve came back with Howie, who had a guilty look on his face.

"He was hiding in the housekeepers' closet," Steve said with disgust. "Okay, kids. You're the detectives here."

But Gil stared at Howie and said, "Didn't you apply for a job as a trail guide?"

"I didn't get it," Howie replied. "I didn't want it, anyway. Too much work, hiking up and down that dumb old trail day after day, picking up trash, telling people they can't touch the precious relics the old-timers dropped during the Gold Rush."

Grandfather looked at Benny. "You think Howie stole the scrapbook and raven and hid them?"

"I think Howie did *some* of that stuff," Benny answered. "But not all of it."

James Alden turned to Howie. "I think my grandson is right. Why don't you tell us your part in this matter."

Howie heaved a sigh. "I'm from Skagway," he began. "All my life I've heard about the Four Rock Miners and their annual reunion. I mean, everybody in town knows about it —"

Gil nodded. "He's right. The reunion has been written up in the newspaper several times. Go on."

Howie continued, "I'm not crazy about

Alaska. I want to go someplace warmer, like California."

"What's stopping you?" asked Violet.

"Money," Howie said simply. "I don't make enough to go to California."

The hotel manager, who'd been listening, remarked, "And you never will, with your attitude. Howie, you don't *want* to work. You're the laziest bellhop I've ever had work for me." He added to the others, "The manager before me hired Howie. I've gone over his references, and none of those people even exist!"

"So I faked my references." Howie shrugged. "Would you hire me if you found out I was fired from my last jobs?"

"You're a bright young man," said Grandfather. "Why cheat and lie and ruin your chances?"

Howie's shoulders drooped. "People like me don't get chances. I needed a break and I found one when you people came."

When the reunion party arrived, he explained, he eavesdropped and learned they were going to the Golden North for dinner. From an old newspaper article, he knew the famous old hotel was where the reunion members passed on the scrapbook and raven statue. Howie knew those items were special, but he didn't know *why*. When he saw James Alden come back with the bundles under his arm, he decided to steal them.

"I took a hotel passkey," Howie said, "and used it to get into Mr. Alden's room."

"But Grandfather was *in* there," Henry stated. "He would have seen you!"

Howie grinned. "I'm good at listening. I could hear water running and figured Mr. Alden was in the bathroom. I hoped he'd have the door closed. He did. I slipped into the room and took the scrapbook and raven off the dresser where he left them and was out in five seconds."

"Was this after you took Steve and Jennifer to their room?" Benny asked.

Howie looked surprised. "Yes, it was. How did you know that?"

"I heard you talking," said Benny. "*I'm*

good at listening, too. What did you do next?"

"I had to move fast," said Howie. "The night clerk was away from his desk, but I didn't know for how long. I couldn't chance leaving my post and going outside to put the raven and scrapbook in my car."

"So you hid them in the lobby?" guessed Miss Parker. "Wasn't that risky?"

"I already knew about the totem pole hiding place," Howie said. "The guy who had this job before me told me about it. I hid the raven in there. But the night guy came back before I could put the scrapbook in, too. So I shut the totem pole panel and stuffed the book in a potted plant."

Grandfather looked disappointed. "You broke into my room and stole things without knowing their value? What did you think you'd get out of that?"

"I want to *be* somebody," Howie said. "I can't do it in this nowhere town."

"You can be somebody anywhere," Miss Parker told him. "But not by lying and stealing. Tell us the rest of your story."

"Well, the night clerk came back and I couldn't get the scrapbook out of the plant, so I left it there overnight." Howie shook his head. "When I came on duty the next morning, it was gone! Somebody had taken it!"

At this point, Monique giggled. Mark wore a silly grin on his face.

"Gotcha!" Mark said to Howie.

"*You* took the scrapbook?" Howie said.

Jessie said, "I knew you two were involved somehow." She whirled on Monique. "You had the scrapbook in your pack the day of the train ride. You got off the train last so no one would see you put the scrapbook on Grandfather's seat."

"Monique, is this true?" Edie Pittman demanded.

"It was just a joke," Monique said. But she looked ashamed. "Maybe it wasn't that funny," she said to Mark.

"Mark also wrote a note telling us to go home," Violet accused. "I recognized his handwriting."

Now Mr. Pittman spoke to his son. "You wrote the Alden kids a nasty note? What is the matter with you?"

"Like we said, it was just a joke," Mark said defensively. "Monique and I were bored. We wanted to have some fun."

"What else did you do?" their mother asked.

Benny knew the answer to that one. "They wrapped up a rock and put it in Miss Parker's pack so she would think she found the raven statue."

Mrs. Pittman looked at her husband. "I think we need to speak to our children."

For once Mr. Pittman wasn't talking loud or complaining. "I don't suppose I've set a very good example for them."

Miss Parker put her hand on Mrs. Pittman's arm. "Don't worry. It's never too late. You have a lovely family. Don't forget it."

Jessie remembered how Monique had given Benny the gold she had panned. Maybe the Pittman kids weren't totally hopeless after all.

She was glad Mark and Monique's part in the "mystery within a mystery" had come to light. But other pieces of the mystery were still in the dark.

"You were listening at our door the night Miss Parker came to us with her letter," Jessie said to Howie.

Howie didn't deny it. "I saw Miss Parker go into Jessie and Violet's room. Then the Wilsons rang for extra ice. The night clerk came upstairs to tell me. I fetched the ice, then went back to the Aldens' door. I heard Miss Parker say something about a letter and 'change his luck.' When she left, I hid behind the drapes."

Violet nodded. "I saw the Wilsons' door close. But I was sure I heard someone outside our door, too."

"You stole the letter as well?" Grandfather asked the bellhop.

"From Miss Parker's bag," Howie said. Now he really sounded regretful. "When you were all in the lobby. Now I knew the Four Rock Miners' things would change my luck. But I didn't have the scrapbook!"

"It turned out the scrapbook wasn't the thing that would change your luck," said Henry. "But it *did* have a clue."

"The photo that fell out," Jessie put in. "You picked it up for me and read what was on the back, didn't you?"

Howie nodded. "The raven was probably the luckiest of the two things, but I still didn't know *how* lucky. It was just an old soapstone carving. I planned to leave it in the totem pole till you guys went home."

By now Gil had cleaned off a large section. The feet and lower body were a beautiful golden yellow. "Looks like the Four Rock Miners had the last laugh on everyone."

The hotel manager took Howie away while he called the police. The glance Howie threw over his shoulder at them showed he was sorry.

"Howie's going to be somebody, all right," said Steve.

Mr. Pittman held the raven. "Looks like we have a decision to make. Do we sell the statue?"

Jennifer and Steve glanced at each other. "We could sure use the money, just starting out," Jennifer said. "But it's such a romantic, fascinating story. If we sell it, we wouldn't be doing what the Four Rock Miners would have wanted."

"Those people are long dead," dismissed Earl Pittman. "This is quite a chunk of gold. Imagine the money it'll bring!"

"I'm far from rich, but I have everything I need," Miss Parker admitted. "What has changed, except we now have a gold statue?"

Grandfather cleared his throat. "Very well put, Miss Parker. I suggest we leave the items to one of the museums here. As Jennifer said, it's a romantic and fascinating story. Let's share it with the world."

Mr. Pittman sighed. "Okay."

The next day, a newspaper reporter came over and took their pictures. The Alden children were interviewed about the mystery and the grown-ups talked about the reunions.

A man from a museum came to claim the

gold raven and scrapbook. He assured them the raven would be cleaned and the Four Rock Miners display would be a popular attraction.

"There'll be a plaque by the display," he said. "With all your names on it."

"Even mine?" asked Benny.

The museum director smiled. "Even yours."

Benny twirled around the totem pole. "Yippee! Now we're *all* somebody!"

"We always have been," said Grandfather. "Sometimes we just don't realize it."

"It's been a great trip," said Jessie. "But we'd better go pack."

They had a long journey home, but she was sure another mystery would be waiting for them!